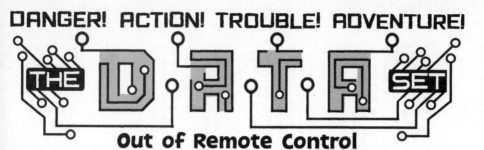

DANGER! ACTION! TROUBLE! ADVENTURE!

THE DATA SET

Out of Remote Control

By Ada Hopper   Illustrated by Graham Ross

LITTLE SIMON
New York London Toronto Sydney New Delhi

LITTLE SIMON

An imprint of Simon & Schuster Children's Publishing Division
1230 Avenue of the Americas, New York, New York 10020
First Little Simon paperback edition November 2017 • Copyright © 2017 by Simon & Schuster, Inc. • All rights reserved, including the right of reproduction in whole or in part in any form. LITTLE SIMON is a registered trademark of Simon & Schuster, Inc., and associated colophon is a trademark of Simon & Schuster, Inc. For information about special discounts for bulk purchases, please contact Simon & Schuster Special Sales at 1-866-506-1949 or business@simonandschuster.com. The Simon & Schuster Speakers Bureau can bring authors to your live event. For more information or to book an event contact the Simon & Schuster Speakers Bureau at 1-866-248-3049 or visit our website at www.simonspeakers.com.
Designed by John Daly. The text of this book was set in Serifa.
Manufactured in the United States of America 1017 MTN 10 9 8 7 6 5 4 3 2 1
Cataloging-in-Publication Data for this title is available from the Library of Congress.
ISBN 978-1-4814-9192-1 (hc)
ISBN 978-1-4814-9191-4 (pbk)
ISBN 978-1-4814-9193-8 (eBook)

CONTENTS

Chapter 1

Is It Saturday Yet?

"Is it Saturday yet?" Cesar asked his friends as they walked to Dr. Bunsen's lab.

Olive shook her head. "Not yet."

Cesar waited a moment. "Is it Saturday yet?"

Olive giggled. "Stop it, Cesar. You're giving me déjà vu!"

Cesar looked confused. "Daze-ya voo?"

"Great phrase, Olive!" cheered Gabe. "Déjà vu is a feeling you get when it seems like you have already done something before."

"Well, I *feel* like this week is moving in slow motion." Cesar groaned. "When is it going to be Saturday?"

The DATA Set needed to finish

their invention for the Newtonburg Science Fest on Saturday.

Laura nudged Cesar forward. "Come on, slowpoke. The Water Zapper is only our best invention yet if we make sure it works."

"Can you imagine turning water into a laser beam?" Olive asked. "There could be farms in the desert, or clean water all around the world, or even on Mars!"

"*If* we get it to work," Gabe reminded them.

Grrr-ROAR-ble! Cesar's stomach made a loud rumble. "Whoa-kay, tummy, I hear you!" As Cesar dug through his pockets for a snack, a big dog bounded out of the bushes. *"RUFF! RUFF!"*

"Whoa!" cried Cesar. He dropped his granola bar on the ground.

CHOMP! The dog snatched up the treat and ran off.

"Hey, you furry thief!" Cesar yelled. "That was a string cheese

peanut butter granola bar, *not* a doggie treat!"

"Peanut butter granola and cheese . . . together?" asked Gabe. The other kids looked disgusted.

"It actually sounds more like

a dog treat than a human treat,"
Olive said. "Maybe Dr. B. will have
some normal food for you."

Then the group laughed. Normal
was the last thing anyone expected
from Dr. Bunsen.

When they arrived at Bunsen's lab, the place was a mess. There were tools and toilet paper everywhere. A half-eaten lunch sat on a countertop next to a bubbling beaker while a cowboy movie blared on the TV. Odd machines buzzed around them.

Laura pinched her nose to block a stinky smell. "Whoa, Dr. B., what happened in here?"

"The life of a traveling scientist, I'm afraid." Dr. Bunsen opened a large suitcase. "I'm speaking before the International Science Council tomorrow."

Then the doctor went into his storage room and returned wearing his x-ray goggles.

"Hey, isn't that where scientists who win the Nobel Prize present their work?" Gabe asked.

But Dr. Bunsen could not hear him over the loud TV. "What did you say?"

"Cesar, can you turn down the volume?" asked Laura.

Cesar grabbed the closest remote control and fumbled with the buttons. All of a sudden, a strange bright glow surrounded the kids and they went *zap*!

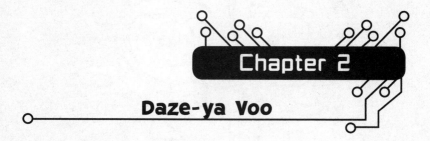

Chapter 2

Daze-ya Voo

"Is it Saturday yet?" Cesar asked. The Data Set were on their way to Dr. Bunsen's lab.

Laura shook her head. "Not yet."

Cesar waited a moment. "Is it Saturday yet?"

Olive giggled. "Stop it, Cesar. You're giving me déjà vu!"

"Hold on," said Gabe. He paused. Something wasn't right. "Does anyone else feel like we've been here before?"

"Don't tell me you're getting déjà vu, too," said Laura.

"I am," replied Gabe. "In fact, Cesar's stomach is about to gurgle."

Grrr-ROAR-ble! Cesar's stomach let out a loud rumble. "Okay, lucky guess! My tummy is always talking. Good thing I packed my . . ."

"String cheese peanut butter granola bar," said Laura, finishing her friend's sentence.

Cesar held up the snack. "Okay, now *that* was weird."

"Look out for that dog in the bushes!" Laura pointed.

Then suddenly a big dog jumped out of the bushes and knocked down Cesar. His snack landed on the sidewalk next to a strange-looking remote control.

The dog sniffed the remote, then grabbed the snack and ran away.

"Hey, you furry thief!" yelled Cesar. "That was a string cheese peanut butter granola bar, *not* a doggie—wait a minute. This *has* happened before. I never forget losing food."

"The remote!" said Laura.

She picked it up and studied it. Cesar came over. "All I did was push that button."

Laura smiled. "You mean the rewind button."

The kids gathered around the device. In any illogical situation, there was only one logical answer.

"Bunsen!" they all said at once.

"This isn't a TV remote—" began Olive.

"Bunsen built a remote control that took *us* back in time!" finished Laura.

Everyone stood in shock until Cesar finally broke the silence. "Do you realize what this means? We can fast-forward to Saturday's competition and see how our invention works!"

"Oh, I can't believe I'm saying this, but I'm in!" said Gabe.

Olive was nervous. "What if something goes wrong?"

"Then we can rewind back!" Laura reminded her. "Don't you want to see if our invention works?!"

"Okay, let's do it!" everyone cheered.

"How do we fast-forward to the exact time?" asked Gabe.

Laura studied the remote. There was a guide button, which usually

listed the channel and showtime
of every TV show. She pressed it.
"This might help."

	1:00 PM	2:00 PM	3:00 PM	4:00
Gabe		Science Fest		
Olive	Soccer Practice	Science Fest		
Laura		Science Fest		
Cesar		Science Fest	Dentist Appointment	

Instantly, a giant grid appeared. It was a channel guide of the DATA Set's weekly schedules!

"There's my soccer practice!" Olive exclaimed.

Cesar frowned. "And there's my dentist appointment."

"And there's the Science Fest!" said Gabe.

Laura selected the Newtonburg Science Fest and pressed the ENTER button.

A bright glow surrounded them and they were thrust into a swirling vortex.

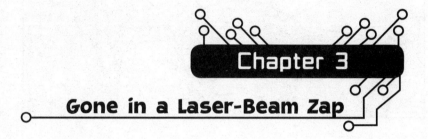

Chapter 3

Gone in a Laser-Beam Zap

ZAP!

The kids appeared inside the Newtonburg Convention Center. There were lots of tables filled with experiments, and the room was crowded with scientists.

"It worked!" cried Laura. "Come on, let's find our station!"

The DATA Set walked past all kinds of gizmos, gadgets, and inventions. There was a hologram projector for dreams, a Venus fly-trap lawn mower, and even a pocket oven that cooked food.

Cesar pointed. "Hey, there's our Water Zapper!"

The invention was on display in a jungle of wilted plants. The DATA Set ran to the device and examined it.

"Do you think it works?" Olive asked.

"It looks like we're about to find out," said Laura.

Two judges stopped at their table.

"What do we have here?" one of the judges asked.

"This is the world's first Water Zapper!" Laura announced proudly. "It can convert water into a laser beam."

"How marvelous!" said the other judge. "Hydro-optic technology is my field of expertise. Can we see how it works?"

"Sure!" said Laura. "Our Water Zapper will bring these wilted plants back to life."

Laura moved the Zapper to a new table. Then she took a deep

breath and pressed the power button.

BZZZZZZZZT! A blue laser beam shot out from the nozzle. The plants immediately started to perk up.

"Remarkable!" said the judges. But as they were writing marks in their notebooks, a strange noise rattled out.

BZZT! BZZT! BZZOOooooommm.

"Oh no!" Laura cried as the Water Zapper started to smoke. She turned it off.

"Hmm, something went wrong, but I can help," said the judge. "Why don't you attend my talk on hydro-ice crystals next week. That's where your invention got watered down."

The other judge nodded.

"You're correct, Dr. Kent. Well, unfortunately that means we won't see a working Water Zapper today."

The DATA Set's hope fell as the judges walked away.

"I can't believe all of our hard work is gone in a laser-beam zap," Cesar groaned.

"Or is it?" Laura's eyes glinted

with excitement. "We have a time remote! We can fast-forward to next week, go to Dr. Kent's talk, then rewind back to here and fix our Water Zapper!"

	6:00 PM	6:30 PM	7:00 PM
	ONE NEWS AT 6 PM		GREEN KNI

7	WHEEL OF MONKEYS		WORLD'S BEST
8	DR. KENT PRESENTS		WHAT'S FOR D

Olive frowned. "But that would be cheating."

Gabe thought about it. "The rules say that we can use any information we need."

"Technically we're not cheating!" exclaimed Laura. She pulled up the guide.

PURPLE NIGHT

"We'll attend the lecture, fix our machine, and be home before you can say 'zap.'"

"Well, I guess we've got nothing to lose," said Olive.

Laura found Dr. Kent's seminar. Then, with a click of the remote, everything became a blur.

THE LOST KEYS	I KNOW YOU ARE, BUT WHAT AM I?
CARTOON WORLD	DREAM CATCHER WILD

Chapter 4

Freeze Waves of the Future

"Whoa." Cesar put his hand on his forehead. "Did that time jump give anyone else brain freeze?"

"It did," Laura admitted dizzily. "But it was worth it. Look!"

As the glow around the kids faded, they stood in front of two large doors. A sign read:

TONIGHT

Dr Kent Presents

HydroCrystals

The Freeze Waves of the Future

"Let's get front-row seats!" Laura exclaimed.

When the entire hall was filled, Dr. Kent stepped onstage. He spoke about hydro-crystals and how they help laser beams. There were graphs, videos, and very long math equations that used every letter in the alphabet.

Laura focused on Dr. Kent's every word. When it was over, she led the DATA Set outside. "Now we can fix our Water Zapper! Let's go back to the Science Fest."

The kids huddled together and Laura pressed rewind.

The familiar glow grew around them, and the world began moving in reverse at lightning speed.

Then the remote control started to smoke! Suddenly the glow clicked to static, and the next thing the kids knew . . . everyone was wearing cowboy hats.

Then the hats disappeared as the ride jolted to a stop. The DATA Set were back at the Science Fest, standing in front of their Water Zapper.

Two judges stopped at their table and smiled.

"What do we have here?" one of the judges asked.

Laura quickly pressed the pause button, and everyone except the kids froze. "Okay, let's try this Water Zapper one more time."

The DATA Set quickly got to work.

Each member fixed different parts of the Water Zapper. When they were done, Laura pressed play, and the room came back to life. This time the laser beam watered the plants and the leaves instantly bloomed.

"Huzzah!" The DATA Set cheered and shared a high five. Unfortunately, the high five made Laura drop the remote. It clunked to the ground and set off a bright glow around them. Then in a flash, they were gone.

Chapter 5

Time Bandits!

The DATA Set landed with a loud *thud* on a hard wooden floor. The floor was bouncing underneath them.

A tall man with a bandana over his face said, "Reach for the sky!"

The kids were aboard an old train in the desert.

Cowboys surrounded them. The tallest one looked very familiar.

"Dr. B.?" Olive exclaimed. "Why are you dressed like a cowboy?"

"Bandit Bunsen's the name. Now empty yer pockets!" the man ordered.

The kids were all wearing Old West outfits too!

"There's been a mistake," Gabe said.

"Your mistake was boarding the train we're robbing," Bunsen growled.

A bandit with scruffy hair stepped forward with a dog by his side. "Hey, boss, we gotta get a move on before the good guys show up."

"Empty yer pockets," Bunsen repeated.

The kids did as they were told.

Laura dropped the remote control into the bag.

"We need to distract them," whispered Gabe. "Cesar, do you have another string cheese peanut butter bar?"

Cesar frowned. "Yes, but it's my last one."

The rest of the DATA Set looked at him like he was crazy.

"Okay, okay," Cesar said. Then he whistled to the dog bandit. "Here, take this!" He threw the treat and the dog blocked off the cowboys to get it.

"Run!" Laura grabbed the bag

from evil Bunsen. The kids raced from train car to train car, with the bandits right behind them. When they reached the caboose, the DATA Set were trapped.

Bandit Bunsen smiled. "End of the line. Now gimme my bag and empty yer pockets."

Quickly, Gabe grabbed the remote from the bag and pressed pause. The entire train and the bandits froze.

"Good thinking!" cheered Laura.

"Yeah! But, what's going on? Where are we?" asked Olive.

"And more important, why are we dressed like this?" asked Cesar.

"Oh no," Gabe groaned and held up the remote. "Do you remember the Western movie that was on the TV at Dr. B.'s? We must have switched over to that channel when the remote dropped."

"You mean we're *in* the movie?" Cesar asked.

Gabe nodded. "I think so."

"That sounds so *not* awesome," said Olive.

"We need to figure out how to get back," said Laura.

She took the remote and pressed the guide button. This time it didn't show the DATA Set's future. Instead, it had a list of other TV shows.

"'*Baking with Bunsen*,'" Gabe read. "'*Mysteries of the Bunsen Kind*.' What sort of guide *is* this?"

ONE	THE MARCH OF THE BUNSEN BEASTS	THE BUNSEN INVASION
2	BAKING WITH BUNSEN	MYSTERIES OF THE BUNSEN KIND
3	DON'T DISTURB THE BUNSEN	BUNSEN RULES THE SCHOOL
4	THE BUNSEN SKY IS FALLING	BUNSEN, I SHRUNK THE BUNSENS
5	A CASE OF THE BUNSEN CLONES	THE BUNSEN HUNTER

"Maybe we should try the 'last' button," Olive suggested. "Wouldn't that take us back home, like switching to the last channel we were on?"

The friends looked at one another and shrugged.

"It's worth a shot," said Laura. She pressed the button and the glow swallowed them again.

Chapter 6

Battlestar Buntastica

When the glow faded, the DATA Set were dressed in space suits. Buttons were blinking under a giant screen that looked out at a dark sky filled with stars.

Suddenly a giant rock flew toward them. Sirens blared a warning signal.

"What is that?!" Cesar cried.

"An asteroid!" Laura shouted as another rock whizzed past. "We're on a starship!"

"The remote must have taken us to the last show Dr. B. watched!" Olive exclaimed. "It's an outer space movie!"

A third asteroid struck the ship as the kids and the remote floated slowly off the floor.

"Warning. Warning. Gravity lost," the ship's computer announced.

"What do we do?" Gabe asked, clinging desperately to a chair.

"We have to fly the ship!" Olive exclaimed. She fastened herself into the pilot's chair as the rest of the crew settled in. Grabbing the steering wheel, Olive turned the ship just in time to narrowly miss another huge rock!

Laura, Gabe, and Cesar clung to their seats with their eyes shut tight.

"It's okay. We're safe!" Olive called out. "But we're not out of trouble yet."

One last asteroid zoomed close.

It was much larger than their ship.
Olive tapped the controls. Then
she pushed the steering wheel
down. The ship dropped, and they
barely missed the enormous rock.

"Great flying, Olive!" said Cesar.
"Where'd you learn to do that?"

"Space camp," said Olive with a
smile.

Then the screen blipped to life,

and a tall blue alien appeared. He had an unruly mop of hair and really big goggles.

"It's Dr. B!" said Cesar.

"You escaped my asteroid trap," Alien Bunsen grumbled. "But you will not escape me. Hand over your ship or meet your doom."

"We are not giving you anything!" Olive said.

The alien chuckled. "Who said anything about 'giving'?"

The emergency siren blared.

Olive checked the controls. "Oh no! He has a tractor beam to capture us!"

The ship lurched to a stop.

"We're trapped!" shouted Gabe. "What can we do?"

"The only thing we *can* do," said Olive. "Change the channel!"

Cesar undid his seat belt and floated in the air to grab the remote. "I have an idea, but I don't know if it will work."

"Anywhere is better than here!" Gabe cried.

Cesar took a deep breath and pressed a button.

Chapter 7

Creatures of the Deep

The kids landed with a *SPLOOSH!* as the glow disappeared. They each wore scuba suits and were surrounded by tropical fish in the ocean.

"Cesar, what button did you press?" Gabe asked.

"The home button," Cesar said.

"I thought it might take us back home."

Laura gazed at all the colorful fish. "Well, at least this channel seems safe."

A low voice echoed around them. "THE DATA SET SWAM DEEPER AND DEEPER."

"Who said that?" Cesar asked.

"THE WATER TURNED DARK AS THE DATA SET TRAVELED FAR BENEATH THE OCEAN WAVES."

"Again! Who was that? And how does he know our name?" Cesar exclaimed.

"I think we dove into a show about deep-sea diving," Laura said.

"Yeah, that voice is the narrator from . . ." Gabe paused. "Oh, what's the name of that show? I can't remember what it's called."

Suddenly the fish all darted away in a swish of white bubbles. The friends looked around at the dark, empty sea.

"Where do you think all the fish went?" Cesar said with a gulp.

"LITTLE DID THE DATA SET KNOW, THE SHARKS HAD COME TO EAT," announced the narrator.

"Did he say sharks?!?" Cesar exclaimed.

"I know this show!" said Gabe. "Each week the host films sharks hunting their prey. It's great."

The kids saw two dark shadows swimming toward them quickly.

"THE UNDERWATER HUNTERS ALWAYS CATCH THEIR PREY."

"Oh no! We're the prey!" Gabe cried. He pointed to some rocks. "Quick! We need to hide!"

The narrator laughed loudly. "SHARKS KNOW THAT THEIR PREY

OFTEN HIDE BEHIND ROCKS."

"Um, okay. Let's try that sea trench!" exclaimed Laura.

The sharks moved closer and came into sight. Instead of the shark's familiar fin, the DATA Set saw something even scarier.

Each beast had fuzzy eyebrows and a mustache. They also wore goggles and lab coats.

"They're Bunsen sharks!" the DATA Set screeched as they swam to the sea trench.

"A SEA TRENCH? REALLY? DOWN IN THE DEEP, THE SHARKS ARE THE MASTERS," the narrator said.

"How about *you* tell us where to hide?" Cesar yelled.

"Hurry! Zap to a different channel before we become their dinner!" Olive yelled.

"But each channel is worse than the last!" said Cesar. "Bandits? Aliens? Sharks? What's next?"

Gabe grabbed the remote and punched in a number. As the glow bubbled around them, the Bunsen sharks were scared away.

"Where are we going?" asked
Olive.

Gabe smiled. "To the safest
channel on TV!"

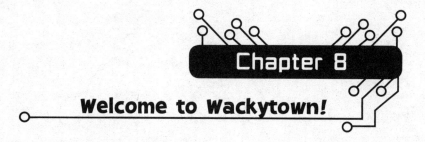

HONK! A cartoon goose blasted a horn in Cesar's ear.

"Gotcha! Ha-ha-ha!" the goose said as it waddled away.

"What is this place?" Cesar looked at his hands. They were rounder than usual and a different color. "Are we . . . cartoons?"

"Welcome to the wild world of Wackytown!" Gabe announced. "This has to be the absolute safest channel in the world. My baby sister watches it all the time and my parents never let her watch TV."

Birds whistled in the dancing trees as forest critters performed tricks like they were in a circus. Everything around the DATA Set was an illustrated cartoon. Then a dark shadow covered the land.

"Hello, hello!" A fluffy monster squeezed them in a giant bear hug. He had purple fur with orange spots and wore Dr. Bunsen–style goggles. "Ready for *sharing* time?"

"Great," Cesar grumbled.

A bunch of toddlers ran from out of nowhere yelling and whooping.

The monster gathered everyone into a circle on the forest floor. "Welcome, friends. I'm Bunster, and today's lesson is about sharing."

HONK! HONK! The goose blasted the horn in Cesar's ear again.

"This may be the safest place, but it's not the quietest," yelled Cesar.

Gabe held the remote to check the guide, but Bunster took it. "Oh, thank you for sharing your toy!"

"Hey! Give me that back right now!" cried Gabe. "It's not a toy! And it's not for sharing!"

"Those aren't the sharing words," Bunster said. "I know! Let's practice sharing in the Ball Pit of Feelings!"

He tossed the remote into a lake filled with different color balls. The children all screamed and jumped in after it.

"No! We have to stop them before they zap to another channel and leave us here forever!" cried Laura.

A determined look crossed cartoon Cesar's face. He leaped into the ball pit and found the remote.

"You heard Bunster. It's *sharing time!*" Quickly, he turned on the remote's guide.

"Select 'The DATA Set Goes Back to Bunsen's Lab,'" said Laura.

Olive gasped. "That's got to be our home!"

Cesar selected the channel, and the DATA Set felt a familiar lurch.

THE DATA SET GOES
BACK TO BUNSEN'S LAB

Chapter 9

The Fabric of Reality

"Is it Saturday yet?" Cesar asked. The DATA Set were on their way to Dr. Bunsen's lab.

The kids looked at one another. They were back to normal and on the sidewalk in Newtonburg.

Olive giggled. "Stop it, Cesar. You're giving me déjà vu!"

"This actually looks like our neighborhood! Does this mean we're home?" Gabe asked.

Carefully, Cesar set his string cheese peanut butter granola bar on the ground. Out of nowhere, a dog

leaped out and snatched the snack.

"Huzzah!" cried Cesar. "I've never been so happy to lose food in my life!"

"We need to find Dr. B.!" Laura said excitedly.

Bunsen was still packing at the lab and waved to the kids. "Ah, my young DATA Set! I was beginning to wonder where you werrrrrrrrrr . . . ouy erehw rednow . . ."

Something wasn't right. The doctor wasn't making sense, and his mouth looked really funny when he talked.

"Dr. B.?" Olive asked.

All of a sudden, Dr. Bunsen started running around the lab in reverse!

"Uh-oh," said Gabe. "Guys . . . something's gone out of control."

The kids watched as their world went from weird, to bad, to *really bad*. Everything in the lab started glitching. The TV came to life and the Bunsen Bandit reached out from the screen!

Through the window, the kids watched the sun rise and set in rapid motion.

"What's going on?" Laura asked as they raced outside. The wind picked up, and leaves flew in weird zigzags. Even the clouds glitched, switching from puffy white to dark and stormy in seconds.

"Can we stop it?" Olive asked desperately.

Laura pressed the stop button on the remote control, but it didn't work. None of the buttons did.

The remote control was dead.

"It's not working!" Laura's face dropped. "What do we do?"

Right then a horrible tearing noise echoed above them.

"Um, what was that?" Cesar asked. "Actually, don't tell me. I don't want to know."

The DATA Set looked up and saw a giant gash in the sky.

Then the narrator's voice boomed. "THE DATA SET WATCHED AS THE WORLD AROUND THEM WAS TORN APART RIGHT BEFORE THEIR VERY EYES."

"Oh no!" Olive gasped. "We broke the world!"

Gabe shook his head. "Not the world. We broke the universe."

Chapter 10

Universal Reboot

The wind picked up as the tear in the sky grew bigger. Everything around the DATA Set had begun to glitch. Houses, trees, and even cows floated upward.

"It's my fault," Laura cried. "I made everyone use the remote."

"We went along with it," said Gabe. "But now we have to fix the universe!"

"Have you checked the batteries?" asked Olive.

Laura opened the back side of the remote. The batteries were glowing.

"I wouldn't mess with those," said Cesar. "You know, once, just once, I'd love for Dr. B. to include the directions for his inventions!"

Laura started to put the back cover on the remote when she noticed some writing. "Wait! There's something printed here."

She held the remote up to her face, trying to make out the tiny print. A tornado of dirt and leaves swirled around them.

"Read faster! The hole is getting larger," cried Cesar.

"There are instructions on how to reboot the remote!" Laura said.

"We can bring the universe back to normal!"

Suddenly a big gust of wind came, lifting Gabe off the ground and into the air. He grabbed Cesar and yelled, "How?"

Laura read the directions aloud. "Hold the power button for five seconds and the remote should reboot."

"Press it already!" yelled Gabe.

Laura held the power button down. "One . . . two," she counted.

The ground under their feet rumbled and cracked. The wind picked up and jerked Gabe right out of Cesar's hands.

"THE DATA SET TRIED TO SAVE THE UNIVERSE . . . BUT WILL IT WORK?" boomed the narrator.

The tear in the sky was glowing.

"Three, four, five!" Laura shouted.

Then, everything went black. It was as if the light of the universe had gone out.

The next thing they knew, the DATA Set were lying on Dr. B.'s floor.

"Is everyone okay?" Laura asked, looking around at the messy lab.

Through a window, the sun was shining brightly as birds chirped a sweet song.

Dr. B. emerged from the storage closet. "DATA Set, what are you doing on the floor?"

"Dr. B.! You're alive and you're not a shark!" Cesar said.

"A shark?" The doctor scratched his head. "Hmm, you may need some rest, Cesar. But not on the lab floor. It's bad for your back. Now maybe you can help me. I'm looking for a TV remote. It's my new invention—"

"Nope!" interrupted the kids all together. "We haven't seen it!"

"But I *did* see your invitation to the International Science Council on your desk!" said Gabe, winking at his friends.

"Yeah, can you tell us about it?" asked Cesar.

"We have all the time in the world!" added Olive.

"Well, the life of a traveling scientist can get out of control sometimes," began Dr. Bunsen. "Follow me. I am packing for a great trip."

As Bunsen left the room, Laura shoved the remote deep into the couch cushions where no one would ever find it.